Inspire us, young artists!
OL

THE WOLF
WHO WANTED TO BE AN

ARTIST

By Orianne Lallemand
Illustrations by Éléonore Thuillier

AUZOU

One fine summer morning, sitting by a waterfall, the Wolf was daydreaming. The birds were singing, the breeze was gently blowing, and the flowers were in bloom.

Suddenly, Mr. Owl interrupted his reverie. "What are you up to, Wolf?" he asked.

"I'm admiring the scenery," replied the Wolf with a sigh. "It's breathtaking, don't you think?"
"Spoken like a true **artist**," answered Mr. Owl, slightly amused by his friend's newly found sensitivity.

3

"Me?" thought the Wolf. "An artist?"
"Come to think of it, I've got talent!" exclaimed the Wolf.
"I've always wanted to **paint**. And from what I heard, artists can be famous!"

So off went the Wolf to buy a canvas, an easel, brushes, and some tubes of paint.
He set up in the shade of an oak tree and got to work!

Working away with his brushes, the Wolf did not notice Wolfette approaching.
"What are you up to, Wolf?" she asked.
"I'm painting," replied the Wolf.
"The colors of the forest and the sound of the waterfall are a true inspiration!"

Wolfette looked at the canvas. All she could see was
a lot of purple and blue.
"My darling Wolf," she started, a little embarrassed,
"I'm not sure that, erm… painting is the right thing for
you. But you'll always be my precious poet!"

"Wolfette is right," exclaimed the Wolf. "I have the soul of a **poet**!"
He found a pencil and some paper, sat down, and started writing.
How enchanting is this summer's day
It really takes my breath away...

The Wolf thought long and hard but couldn't come up with any more rhymes.

Deep in his thoughts, the Wolf suddenly heard a voice right behind him. "Why are you sitting here, as still as a statue?" asked Valentine.

The Wolf jumped up.

"A **sculptor**!" he shouted. "I'll be a very talented sculptor."

Miss Yeti volunteered to pose for the Wolf. Off they went to his garden where he carefully shaped the clay in his paws. As he put the finishing touches, the Wolf admired his work.
"Come and have a look," he told Miss Yeti.

Miss Yeti took one look at the
statue and started wailing.
"I look like an elephant!"
she cried.
"Are you trying to be funny,
Wolf? Well let me tell you,
you have absolutely no
talent as a sculptor!"

She trampled the statue before stomping off into the forest.

"**Funny Wolf**?" he repeated. "That's it, I was meant to be a comedian! I do love making people laugh!"

The cheerful Wolf set up a stage in the forest and rehearsed for his show.
The passers-by were so fascinated by what he was doing, they stopped to listen.

Unfortunately, nobody laughed at his jokes.
In fact, our poor Wolf was booed off stage before the end of his show.

15

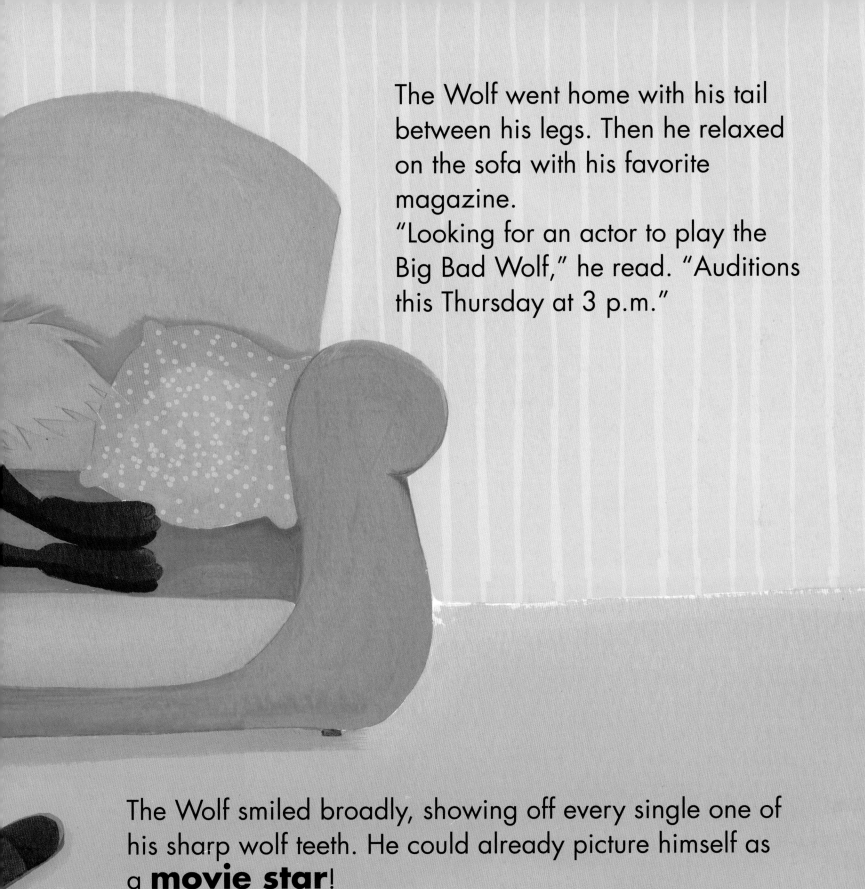

The Wolf went home with his tail between his legs. Then he relaxed on the sofa with his favorite magazine.
"Looking for an actor to play the Big Bad Wolf," he read. "Auditions this Thursday at 3 p.m."

The Wolf smiled broadly, showing off every single one of his sharp wolf teeth. He could already picture himself as a **movie star**!

The next day, the Wolf made sure he was on time for the audition.
But when he opened the door the Wolf got a terrible fright.
"**AAAHHHHHH!**" he howled. "Those wolves are terrifying!"

Hearing his howls, the producer ran out of his office to take a closer look at this amazing wolf.

"You're not scary at all," he declared. "But you have an amazing voice!"

"You should be a singer," he continued. "You'd be all the rage!"

"Oh, thank you," said the Wolf. "I do love singing in the shower!"

The Wolf rushed home and announced the news to his friends.
"I'm going to be a **rock star**," he told them. "Who wants to be in my band?"

"Me!" shouted Big Louis. "I'll be the drummer!"
"And I can play the saxophone," said Alfred.
"I'm a great musician!" declared Valentine. "I can play the electric guitar!"
"And I can write the songs," suggested Joshua.

"What about us?" asked Wolfette and
Miss Yeti.
"My darlings," crooned the Wolf.
"You will be our backup singers."

"And I'll be the lead singer," said the Wolf. "I have an incredible voice. Listen!"
And he started singing. His friends were stunned. The Wolf really did have talent!

lalalalalaaaa

"We'll meet here tomorrow," the Wolf told his friends. "Bring your instruments. And when we've rehearsed, we'll put on a show!"

The band was named The Rocking Wolves. They put in a lot of work, writing the songs, composing the music, setting up the stage and making lighting and sound adjustments. Most importantly, they rehearsed every single day.

When everything was ready for the concert, they put up posters all over the forest. "Open invitation for The Rocking Wolves concert. Fantastic music and a great time guaranteed!" they read.

The Rocking

The big night arrived at last. The Wolf made his entrance. He took a deep breath and started singing. At the end of the first song, there was complete silence... Followed by a thunder of applause.

"One more, one more!" shouted the audience.

Phew! The Wolf sighed with relief. The band lit up the stage and their concert was an amazing success.

The next day, The Rocking Wolves were on the front page of all the newspapers. And they were invited to play in Paris, New York, and Rio!

Rolling Stone

"I've always been an artist at heart"

THE WOLF
Leader of the Rocking Wolves

Exclusive interview

The Wolf replied to all the invitations:
"Thank you, you're very kind," he said.
"It's great being a **star** but I have way
more interesting things to do, right here at
home."

Managing Director: Gauthier Auzou
Senior Editor: Laura Levy
Layout: Annaïs Tassone, Alice Vignaux
Project Management for the English edition: Ariane Laine-Forrest
Translation from French: Susan Allen Maurin
Original title: Le loup qui voulait être un artiste

Printed and bound in China, January 2017.

WHO'S AFRAID OF THE BIG BAD WOLF?

Meet the Wolf! His quirky, tongue-in-cheek humor and fun-loving personality is perfect for children. And his lively adventures appeal to both early readers and parents alike.

The Wolf is now a household name in France, thanks to the fundamental concepts—such as accepting yourself, birthdays, and history—subtly woven into each story. Welcome the Wolf into your home, too!

Being naughty has never been so good!

In the same series:

   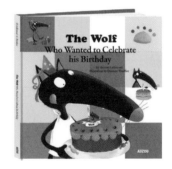

Also available:

 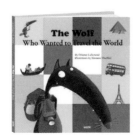